VIOLENCE AND SOCIETY™

BOMB SCARES

AMY STERLING CASIL

ROSEN PUBLISHING®
New York

Published in 2009 by The Rosen Publishing Group, Inc.
29 East 21st Street, New York, NY 10010

Library of Congress Cataloging-in-Publication Data

Casil, Amy Sterling.
Bomb scares / Amy Sterling Casil. — 1st ed.
   p.cm.—(Violence and society)
Includes bibliographical references.
ISBN-13: 978-1-4042-1791-1 (library binding)
1. Bomb threats. 2. Bombing investigation. I. Title.
HV8079.B62C37 2008
363.325—dc22

2007048650

Manufactured in Malaysia

On the cover: A member of New York City's bomb squad investigates a threat in Times Square.

CONTENTS

INTRODUCTION

James Wilson, chief assistant prosecutor in Passaic County, N.J., and law enforcement officers in the town of Wayne, N.J., announce the arrest of five students in connection with the June 2007 Wayne Valley High School bomb scare.

On the night of June 12, 2007, final exams were about to start at New Jersey's Wayne Valley High School. At about 11:00 PM, surveillance cameras on the school's second floor silently recorded two mysterious hooded figures as they hid four dark packages in student lockers.

The next morning as school started, a student saw a strange-looking wire sticking out of one of the lockers and called for help. School security officers found four bombs and fuses fastened together with masking tape inside the lockers. Final exams were immediately cancelled and nearly 1,500 students were evacuated as the bomb squad removed the devices from the school.

Police captain Paul Ireland told the *Bergen Record* that the devices resembled half sticks of dynamite. The *Record* also reported that bomb squad commander Dave Michelini told the Wayne school board that if the devices had exploded at the school, he could almost bet that people would have been hurt. The devices turned out to be smoke bombs containing gunpowder—not dynamite—and in Michelini's opinion, they would have exploded in a large fireball and a lot of smoke. The sheriff's bomb squad was able to detonate the smoke bombs safely at the Passaic County bomb squad range.

Police reviewed hours of security videotapes to determine who had planted the smoke bombs. Tapes from the previous day showed a group of undisguised students carrying black bags containing the smoke

bombs and hiding them in various locations around the school. Soon, five students identified on the tapes were arrested.

Wayne Valley is one of two high schools in Wayne, New Jersey. With 1,500 students and a broad range of sports and other activities, it could be like any other American high school. Before the bomb scare, nobody thought there was anything sinister about the name of the school newspaper: *Smoke Signals*

The attorney for one of the students arrested under suspicion of planting the smoke bombs told the *Record* that his client was a straight-A student who had never been accused of nor involved in any violation of the law. The five suspects, if charged and convicted, could face up to ten years in prison. (As of the writing of this book, the investigation was still ongoing.)

Ten days after the bomb scare, the senior class of Wayne Valley High School prepared to graduate. Their graduation ceremony was moved inside the school's gym for security reasons, leaving little room for many parents and friends. While waiting outside, frustrated eighteen-year-old student Anthony Purcell told the *Bergen Record* that his best friend was originally accused of the crime and questioned for hours. Purcell's friend had been the student who told school officials he had seen a fuse or wire hanging out of a second-floor locker. He saved the school, Purcell told the *Record*, but they treated him like a criminal.

A sixteen-year-old sophomore told the *Record* that she thought the school wasn't secure. She echoed the statements of many other students to the *Record* that security had to be improved. Many expressed fears of bombs exploding inside the school in the future, even though this incident had turned out to be a smoke bomb prank.

From senior pranks to real bombs, from scares at sports events, airports, or bus stations, to war-torn countries where unexploded bombs or IEDs (improvised explosive devices) threaten innocent lives, bomb scares impact everyone's lives.

CHAPTER ONE
What Is a Bomb Scare?

A bomb scare doesn't have to involve a real bomb. Some bomb scares are the result of hoaxes or pranks. Devices that look very dangerous can actually turn out to be less dangerous when trained professionals examine them. The Wayne Valley High School smoke bombs had, at first, looked like four sticks of dynamite to school officials.

High schools and colleges are some of the most frequently targeted sites for bomb scares. According to former Alabama police captain Jim Smith, author of *A Law Enforcement and Security Officers' Guide to Responding to Bomb Threats*, it is common for schools to receive bomb threats when tests are scheduled. Smith also said that the majority of school bomb threats are made via the telephone, which will come as no surprise to most students and teachers.

A typical school bomb scare occurred in Milwaukee, Wisconsin, in April 2000. Seventeen-year-old Milwaukee student Tyler Despot was afraid of failing a geometry test. He went to a phone booth after school and, according to the *Milwaukee Sentinel*, told his school's after-hours answering machine, "There is a bomb in your school. It will blow Thursday afternoon." After his voice was quickly recognized, Despot was arrested, charged with making the threat, and tried. He pled guilty to the crime, paid a fine of several thousand dollars, and was sentenced to ninety days in jail and two years of probation.

Other types of bomb threats tend to be made in person, via e-mail, or through the U.S. mail. One of the most frightening types of bomb threat is a letter or package sent through the mail. Today, these suspicious packages could possibly contain biological weapons that can spread infectious diseases.

One famous case of bombs sent through the U.S. mail involved Theodore Kaczynski, also known as the Unabomber. He sent package and letter bombs to people for seventeen years. Kaczynski's packages killed three people and injured twenty-nine others. This case contributed to a growing fear of opening unfamiliar packages or letters. This fear grew even stronger after the anthrax scare of 2001.

Biological bombs containing the dangerous disease anthrax were sent following the September 11, 2001, terrorist attacks. The September 2001 anthrax scare began with the mailing of at least seven letters infected with deadly anthrax spores from a post office in Trenton, New Jersey. Twenty-two people became infected with anthrax, and five of them died. The letters contained a strain of weaponized, or deadly, anthrax that was made in a biological laboratory. The anthrax scare remains a mystery. No suspect has been apprehended as of the writing of this book.

Although the anthrax letters were real, experts from the Federal Bureau of Investigation (FBI) assure the public that the majority of bomb threats made through the mail are hoaxes. Most FBI offices in American towns and cities receive dozens of reports of such bomb scares a week. Most suspected anthrax letters have turned out to be envelopes filled with baby powder or powdered sweetener. They are often sent as pranks, and sometimes they are intended to frighten and intimidate the recipient.

Unabomber Theodore Kaczynski leaves a Montana courtroom in the custody of two federal officers after his arrest in April 1996.

FBI and local law enforcement officials agree that it doesn't matter whether bomb threats are fakes or hoaxes, or incorporate real explosive devices. First responders—who are typically local firefighters, police, or specialized bomb squad technicians—must always act as if the threats are real until their investigations are complete. The fear that results from a hoax can be as harmful and frightening as the fear resulting from a real bomb.

History of Bombs and Bomb Scares

Bombs are used for many purposes today. Originally, they were primarily used for war. The Chinese invented gunpowder, which was the first powerful explosive material. Gunpowder's earliest use in China dates to the year 850, when it was used to set buildings or land on fire. By the twelfth and thirteenth centuries, Chinese armies were constructing gunpowder rockets that would explode upon impact. They also created exploding bombs, and they fired ordnance (explosive weapons) from bronze cannons. They built grenades, smoke bombs, and even gas bombs that would explode and poison enemy soldiers.

In Europe, the earliest bombs were grenades. During the seventeenth century, grenades were created for use by grenadiers, who were special troops trained for sieges (attacks upon cities with stone walls protecting them). Grenades were heavy iron spheres with a fuse or wick (like a candle). They were filled with gunpowder that exploded when the fuse ignited it, sending shards of hot and exploding metal—called shrapnel—flying through the air.

One of history's most famous bomb scares took place in England in November 1605. The "Gunpowder Plot" was the result

In this traditional engraving, British Gunpowder Plot conspirator Guy Fawkes tries to ignite gunpowder beneath the British Parliament on November 5, 1605.

of religious conspirators plotting to blow up Parliament, England's government building. They also hoped to kill everyone in the House of Lords and King James I.

The most famous of these conspirators was Guy Fawkes. He filled an entire room under Parliament with gunpowder. Modern explosives experts think that if Fawkes had managed to ignite the gunpowder, most of the Parliament building would have been destroyed in the blast.

Fawkes was caught before he could set off the explosion, and he and the other conspirators were executed. The Gunpowder Plot became so famous in the United Kingdom that November 5 is a national holiday—it is called Guy Fawkes Day, or Bonfire or Fireworks Day.

The Gunpowder Plot was an early example of a political bomb scare that, over time, became more common. In 1801, French leader Napoleon Bonaparte was nearly killed by a bomb that political opponents placed underneath his carriage. In 1881, tsar Alexander II of Russia died after two young anarchists threw two bombs at his carriage. Anarchists were politically motivated people of the nineteenth and early twentieth centuries who wanted to eliminate the government.

Bomb scares, political bombings, and bomb extortion (threats for money) became common in the United States around 1900,

NYPD bomb squad members investigate a bomb scare on July 3, 2002, near the entrance to the Holland Tunnel.

and they began in New York City. New York is the home of the nation's oldest police bomb squad, which celebrated its 100th anniversary in 2003. The New York Police Department (NYPD) bomb squad's first assignments came around 1900, when a gang called the Black Hand threatened businesses and families in Italian neighborhoods with bombings if they didn't pay money. The NYPD bomb squad stopped the Black Hand. Later, the squad faced German spies and bomb threats during World War I.

The next type of bomb threat in the United States came from political radicals or anarchists, who began using bombs to achieve their goals. In 1919, anarchist bombs exploded in eight U.S. cities. The next year, they put a gigantic bomb in a horse-drawn wagon in front of the J. P. Morgan Bank on New York's Wall Street. The bomb exploded, killing forty people.

In the 1930s, as the Depression (a time of severe economic hardship for many people in the United States) grew worse, bomb attacks continued. Although few people were actually harmed, stink bomb attacks in movie theaters frightened many people. The suspects in the stink bomb attacks were the theaters' own projectionists. They were on strike against theater owners, and they believed that the stink bombs would highlight their complaints about wages and working conditions.

The phrase "Mad Bomber," which today is heard in cartoons and jokes, began with a real series of crimes. In 1940, a string of bomb attacks began that would terrorize New York City for the next sixteen years. The Mad Bomber turned out to be an unemployed man named George Metesky, who was finally arrested in 1956. Metesky's motive for the bombings was resentment against his former employer after being hurt on the job.

The Mad Bomber wrote threatening letters to newspapers and placed his homemade pipe bombs in theaters, subway stations, and phone booths. Although many people were injured in the Mad Bomber's blasts, no one was directly killed.

The Reality Today

A small bomb in the nineteenth century could blow up a carriage, kill its horses, and kill or injure several people. Today, dirty

New York City's "Mad Bomber," George Metesky, sits behind bars in January 1957 after his arrest.

bombs—or bombs containing chemical weapons—can spread deadly radiation and thus potentially kill hundreds of thousands of people.

On average, police bomb squads in large cities like Los Angeles respond to more than a thousand bomb threats a year. About 24 percent of the bomb threats in Los Angeles turn out to be real explosive devices, not threats or hoaxes. Police bomb squads use many different tools and technologies to cope

with real threats. They also educate the public about bomb threat safety and work with other first responders to ensure everyone's safety during a threat—real or hoax. Bomb squad professionals also use their extensive training and experience to identify and respond to the risk factors when a bomb threat is received or a suspected bomb is discovered.

CHAPTER TWO

When Threats Are Real

The most terrifying type of bomb scare is one where a real bomb is in danger of exploding, or, worst of all, does explode. While police bomb squads do everything in their power to prevent bombs from exploding, sometimes there is no time to act before disaster strikes. At other times, explosive devices take forms that most people wouldn't recognize as dangerous.

In 2004, plastic soda bottles gained popularity as home-made explosives. Pranksters came up with the idea of putting soda bottle bombs in mailboxes so they could watch and even film the explosive results. Today, more than two hundred videos on the video-sharing Web site YouTube show people making explosive devices from plastic soda bottles and common household chemicals. Soda bottle bombs aren't an innocent prank. They can injure or potentially kill their creators, the unlucky mailbox owners, or innocent passers-by.

Captain Jim Smith, author of the *Law Enforcement and Security Officers' Guide to Responding to Bomb Threats*, reported that in 2004, an eighty-one-year-old New Jersey man saw a passenger in a car on his street toss a soda bottle out of the window. He bent down to pick up what he thought was a harmless piece of trash and was critically injured when it exploded in his face. According to the *Law Enforcement Guide*, the elderly victim said, "I can't believe this happened just because I was trying to keep the street clean."

An Oklahoma City firefighter walks through the devastation after the April 19, 1995, bombings at the Alfred P. Murrah Federal Building.

Also in 2004, two six-year-old boys from the Chicago area were injured when they picked up a soda bottle bomb left on the grounds of their apartment complex by a pair of teens who were later convicted of the crime. The boys were under their parents' supervision, learning how to clean up their neighborhood.

Authentic bombs placed in locations where people could be hurt or killed are much more serious than prank bombs.

Today, real bombs are planted by bombers who are politically motivated; these bombers tend to be terrorists or activists. Others may be acting based upon many different types of criminal motivation. Some bombers can be mentally ill like the Unabomber,

10 QUESTIONS TO ASK
A BOMB SAFETY EXPERT

1. Does our school have a safety plan for bomb scares and other disasters?

2. What should I do if I see a suspicious package or backpack left somewhere?

3. How can I establish a safety plan with my family in case of a bomb scare?

4. What can I do if my school is affected by a bomb scare?

5. What kinds of bombs are likely to be prevalent in the future?

6. What can students do to prevent bomb scares at their school?

7. Do stores and businesses get threatened by bomb scares?

8. What are the different types of bombs and how can they be recognized?

9. Are there videos or books on how explosive ordnance disposal (EOD) or bomb-sniffing dogs get trained?

10. Can I read a book or see a video about how bomb squads prepare for bomb scares and real bombs?

Ted Kaczynski. Kaczynski's mental illness allowed his brother to recognize unusual phrases written in the 1995 "Manifesto" Kaczynski wrote, which was published in the *New York Times* and the *Washington Post*, leading to Kaczynski's eventual capture and conviction.

Real Bomb Types and Bombers

Major bomb attacks destroy entire buildings and kill many people. Car or truck bombs often play a role in such attacks. The September 11, 2001, terrorist attacks on the World Trade Center in New York City are so well known that they have overshadowed the earlier 1993 terrorist attack on the twin towers. In the 1993 attack, a 1,500-pound car bomb was detonated in the underground parking area beneath Tower One. The car bomb was intended to cause Tower One to collapse into Tower Two, and it was also meant to release a poisonous gas, sodium cyanide, into the city's air, potentially killing hundreds of thousands of people. The bomb severely damaged Tower One, injuring more than one thousand people and killing six, but the cyanide gas burned up in the explosion and poisoned no one. Ten Islamic terrorists were eventually convicted of the attack and are currently serving life sentences in federal prison.

Another very large car bomb exploded outside of the Alfred P. Murrah Federal Building in Oklahoma City, Oklahoma, on the morning of April 19, 1995. The Murrah Building was almost completely destroyed, more than 800 people were injured, and 168 people were killed. The enormous blast measured a 3.0 on the Richter earthquake scale in communities as far as 16 miles (25.74 kilometers) away, and it was heard for a much greater distance. Bomber Timothy McVeigh was convicted of

the crime and received the death penalty. A second conspirator, Terry Nichols, is serving a life term without the possibility of parole in a high-security federal prison. Until the September 11, 2001, attacks on the World Trade Center and the Pentagon, the Oklahoma City bombing was the most destructive act of terrorism ever committed on American soil. Both U.S. citizens, Nichols and McVeigh viewed the attack as a political statement about what they believed to be the corrupt U.S. government.

Here is an overview of the various types of popular bombs:

Pipe Bombs

A pipe bomb is a simple type of explosive device that consists of a sealed section of metal pipe filled with explosives, attached to a detonation device. Dylan Klebold and Eric Harris, the teens who carried out the Columbine High School massacre on April 20, 1999, in Colorado made and used at least four pipe bombs in addition to their shooting rampage.

Closed Bombs

Closed bombs contain any type of explosive that can be concealed in a box, bag, backpack, or briefcase. They usually have a timed or remote detonation device. Unusual closed bombs have been concealed in laptop computers, and, in one case, a running shoe. Today, people must remove their shoes while passing through airport security because Richard Reid, the so-called "shoe bomber," was prevented from blowing up an American Airlines flight with plastic explosives in his shoes in December 2001. The March 11, 2004, train bombings in Madrid, Spain, that injured more than 2,000 people and killed 191 others were the result of thirteen

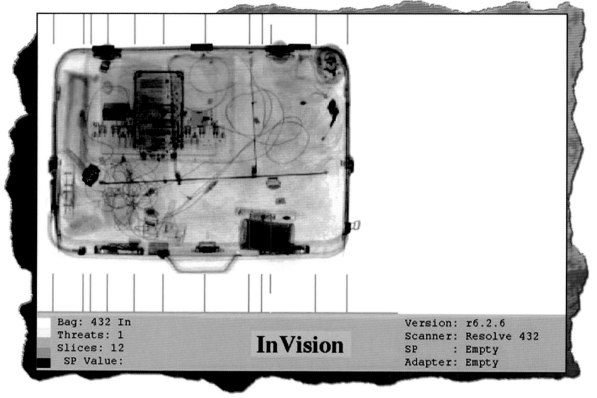

Bag: 432 In		Version: r6.2.6
Threats: 1	**In Vision**	Scanner: Resolve 432
Slices: 12		SP : Empty
SP Value:		Adapter: Empty

Airport security systems today provide images similar to this X-ray image from 1995 of a "can bomb" concealed in luggage.

explosive-filled backpacks placed by Islamic terrorists on busy commuter trains.

Letter and Package Bombs

Letter or package bombs are explosive devices placed inside packages or large envelopes. The trigger mechanisms of these bombs cause an explosion when a package is opened. Ted

How Bombs Are Discovered

In 1936, the New York City bomb squad became the first agency to use X-rays to see inside packages that could contain bombs. Today, X-rays and similar technology are used in sophisticated ways to detect explosive devices of all types, from incendiary to biological and chemical. Terahertz radiation is a new technology under development that can use a unique type of radiation to see at a distance the fingerprint of virtually any type of explosive or other dangerous material.

Ion technology is another new form of bomb detection that has begun to be used in airports and high-security buildings. Handheld ion wands or larger scanners can detect tiny particles of chemicals that are uniquely found in bombs, aiding in detection. Trace detection is a similar chemical process that can identify vehicle emissions or find a human convection plume, which is an invisible trail of chemicals that could show if a person is carrying an explosive device.

In addition to technology, the human training that goes into security, safety, and bomb detection and identification is invaluable. Since 1981, the FBI has trained bomb technicians at its Hazardous Devices School (HDS) in Huntsville, Alabama. Local police officers who serve on FBI-certified bomb squads have all received training in Huntsville to cope with bomb scares and threats. They learn how to neutralize real bombs—exploding them in a safe manner, or defusing them before detonation.

An Austrian detective examines the remains of a letter bomb that exploded in a postal box in Graz, Austria, in 1995.

Kaczynski injured twenty-three people and killed three more by sending letter and package bombs through the U.S. mail.

Bottle Bombs

Some people are now putting explosive household chemicals inside plastic soda bottles as a joke or prank. Other types of bottle bombs include glass bottles filled with acid, black powder,

and sharp objects such as nails, and Molotov cocktails, which are bottles containing a highly flammable liquid such as gasoline.

Car Bombs and Open Bombs

These undisguised bombs rely upon speed, or upon concealment and remote detonation. Open bombs are constructed of highly explosive materials and are usually detonated at a distance by cell phone, pager, or radio device. IEDs, or improvised explosive devices, are homemade bombs developed during the recent conflicts and wars in the Middle East. Some open IEDs can hide in plain sight until they are detonated as military vehicles pass by. Car and truck bombs can be parked and detonated remotely, or they are driven up to a location and then detonated. Sometimes, the driver remains inside the vehicle and is killed in the explosion; this is known as a suicide bombing. Many very serious bombings have been the result of car or truck bombs, such as the 1999 Oklahoma City bombing and the 1993 World Trade Center bombing.

Bomb-Sniffing Dogs

Dogs can be invaluable partners to human bomb squad professionals in detecting bombs and helping to save lives. Bomb-sniffing dogs are also known as explosive ordnance disposal (EOD) canines. A bomb-sniffing dog can cost up to $15,000, which includes a month or more of specialized, intensive training. Dogs can be trained to sniff the distinctive odors in bombs because their sense of smell is twenty to forty times better than that of humans. Typically, bomb-sniffing dogs are trained to recognize about twenty-five different distinct odors that are given off by

Bomb Scares

Former U.S. Air Force tech sergeant Jamie Dana and her bomb-sniffing dog, Rex, walk near her home in Pennsylvania in 2006.

the thousands of different explosive devices that have been developed.

Bombs are a constant threat in Iraq and other war-torn countries. Hundreds of bomb-sniffing dogs have served with U.S. military security forces in Iraq. One famous bomb-sniffing dog from Iraq is Rex, a six-year-old German shepherd.

Rex's owner is former U.S. Air Force tech sergeant Jamie Dana, who was injured on duty in Iraq by a bomb that wasn't successfully defused before it exploded. When Dana woke up in the hospital, she was mistakenly told that Rex had been killed in the blast. Later she learned that Rex was safe.

As she prepared to return home, she thought it would be nice to take the dog with her. However, Dana discovered that she couldn't officially adopt Rex because the air force had spent a lot of money training him. They said they couldn't afford to let him go.

It took an act of U.S. Congress proposed by Dana's congressman to allow the rules to be changed. After this, Rex was taken to Dana's Pennsylvania home to retire. Both she and Rex were celebrated by Congress and recognized for their heroism during the president's State of the Union Address in 2006.

CHAPTER THREE
Fake Bombs and Hoaxes

S ome individual bombers suffer from mental illness. Like New York's Mad Bomber in the 1950s, they lack the ability to judge the effects of their actions. Then there are pranksters who mean no real harm but misjudge how frightening and traumatic a bomb scare can be to people who aren't in on the joke.

Dr. Jon G. Allen wrote in *Coping with Trauma* that terrorist attacks such as bomb scares and threats do not have to result in death to cause intense fear and trauma. A trauma reaction is a natural response to sudden stress and fear. It can include a period of sleeplessness, as well as depression, worry, fear, and hyper vigilance, or extreme alertness for danger. Trauma reactions can last for weeks, and sometimes months, following the traumatic event. Physical symptoms can also occur. These symptoms include increased heartbeat and body temperature, or unexpected weight loss or gain. A stress or trauma disorder is more serious and longer lasting than a trauma reaction. Immediate counseling and sometimes just talking about the bomb scare or threat can help a person overcome fear and the trauma reaction.

Even such efforts as art projects can cause trauma. People experienced trauma reactions after a Seattle, Washington, art project turned into a bomb scare. Jason Sprinkle, a self-described "art warfare guerilla," frightened many people in Seattle on July 15, 1996. Sprinkle parked a broken-down truck

that he had decorated near a downtown park. According to the Online Encyclopedia of Washington State History (http://www.historylink.org), the words "Timberlake Carpentry Rules (The Bomb!)" were painted on the side of the truck. A nine-block square area was evacuated, and Sprinkle was arrested. He received a fine and twelve months' probation. Despite people's fears, Sprinkle insisted that the truck was a piece of artwork, not a bomb threat.

Artists Sean Stevens and Peter Berdovsky answer reporters' questions about the Boston bomb scare caused by their electronic *Aqua Teen Hunger Force* creations in February 2007.

An electronic "Mooninite" advertising the *Aqua Teen Hunger Force* adult cartoon caused a bomb scare in February 2007.

Aqua Teen Hunger Force

On January 31, 2007, an ad campaign for the adult-oriented cartoon *Aqua Teen Hunger Force* terrified Boston residents and shut down a major highway, a bus station, and parts of the city's subway system. Two artists, Peter Berdovsky and Sean Stevens, placed small electronic boxes near roads and under bridges to promote the Cartoon Network show. Other similar devices were placed in ten other cities, but Boston was the only place where the square black boxes featuring flashing magnetic lights were interpreted as potential terrorist bombs.

An advertising executive told the *Boston Globe* that the electronic boxes were part of a "viral marketing" campaign designed to reach twenty-something viewers of the cartoon. A viral marketing campaign consists of nontraditional, person-to-person advertising instead of television commercials or newspaper or magazine advertisements. Some younger Boston residents, such as twenty-two-year-old design student Todd Vanderlin, had seen the boxes and recognized them as advertisements. But a subway passenger who had never heard of the cartoon spotted one of the boxes in a seemingly suspicious location under a support column and alerted authorities. The discovery of more boxes launched a twelve-hour evacuation and bomb detection effort that eventually encompassed most

of downtown Boston. Meanwhile, the scare reached a national news audience.

Donna Manca, a native New Yorker, was reminded of the September 11, 2001, terrorist attacks by the strategically placed advertisements. She told the *Boston Globe* that she was very frightened. Manca said, "That's awful. It's a terrible, terrible thing to do." Lynn Wilcott, an employee at Massachusetts General Hospital, commented to the *Globe* that "a package is a suspicious package, no matter how cute it is."

The two artists who originally placed the light-emitting advertisements were initially charged with crimes related to the incident; the charges were later dropped. Turner Broadcasting Network, the parent company of the Cartoon Network, agreed to pay the city of Boston and the state of Massachusetts to cover costs related to the hoax. The executive in charge of the Cartoon Network resigned in connection with the controversy.

Pranks, Hoaxes, and Jokes

Bomb pranks, hoaxes, and jokes seem funny to their perpetrators but can terrify everyone else. Bomb hoaxes can also be perpetrated for serious, if misguided, reasons. For example, in September 2006, a sixty-three-year-old priest who objected to religious symbols of crosses and images of Christ portrayed in pop artist Madonna's performances tried to stop a scheduled series of her concerts in Amsterdam, Holland. He thought the best way to stop the concerts was to phone in a bomb threat to the police. As bomb fears began to spread, the hoax was discovered and the priest was arrested for making a false bomb threat. Dutch authorities said that due to his age and lack of criminal record, the priest was likely to receive light punishment.

In July 2004, a bomb threat on United Airlines Flight 840 from Sydney, Australia, to Los Angeles, California, forced the flight to turn around and return to Sydney Airport, dumping all of its fuel and landing on a special strip flanked by fire trucks and ambulances. Frightened passengers and airline officials soon learned that the threat was a hoax. The word "bomb" had been written on an airsickness bag that was left in a suspicious location.

Employees and customers wait in a Hutchinson, Kansas, grocery store's parking lot after an extortion bomb threat in August 2007.

United Airlines and Australian officials were justifiably on edge in this case. Terrorist bomb threats had been made only days earlier against Australia's airports and tourists in an attempt to force the country to withdraw its troops from the war zone in Iraq.

Extortion bomb threats are primarily motivated by the desire to obtain money from fearful targets. In August 2007, an FBI investigation began into twenty-four extortion bomb threats made to stores located in seventeen U.S. states. The threats targeted local branches of major stores like Wal-Mart, as well as smaller grocery stores and banks. A male telephone caller demanded that local store management send money to overseas bank accounts, or he would detonate bombs at the stores, killing employees and customers. Terrified employees at one of the Wal-Mart stores wired payments totaling $10,000 to stop the bomb threat. Employees at another supermarket responded with a $3,000 payment. Soon after, copycat callers were arrested attempting to imitate the crimes. The original bomb threat caller, who was suspected to be someone who had previously committed similar crimes, has not been apprehended.

Suspicious Activities or Items: Innocent Explanations

With increased awareness of bomb threats following the tragedy of September 11, 2001, and other more recent attacks in Great Britain and other parts of Europe, airport security, law enforcement personnel, and members of the public are on alert more than ever before. This alertness is important to everyone's safety. However, some suspected bomb scares turn out to have very innocent explanations. Neither pranks nor hoaxes, they are simple human misunderstandings.

With steady increases in airport security and cautionary procedures, these misunderstandings frequently occur at airports. On September 3, 2004, a misplaced bag filled with cosmetics caused a two-hour shutdown of Ontario International Airport in southern California. Two thousand waiting passengers and airport employees were evacuated as a result. The next day, four terminals at nearby Los Angeles International Airport, one of the world's busiest airports, were shut down after two incidents. First, a passenger's flashlight battery exploded in a

MYTHS AND FACTS

Myth: Most bomb scares are caused by terrorists.

Fact: The majority of bomb scares are caused by pranksters or hoaxers (including students) and extortionists (people trying to get money through the scare).

Myth: Bombs are easy to spot.

Fact: Bombs are often made out of ordinary materials such as plastic soda bottles. They can also be concealed in common items like packages, envelopes, and backpacks.

Myth: Bomb scares are rare.

Fact: Urban police departments receive more than one thousand reports of suspected bombs a year. About 20 to 25 percent of the time, the suspected bombs turn out to be real explosive devices.

transportation safety worker's hand as the passenger's bag was being screened. The second incident occurred in the next terminal, where another passenger, frustrated at the delays caused by the battery explosion, ran past security checkpoints. Together, both incidents caused massive evacuations and shutdowns, delaying more than thirty outbound flights and delaying or canceling seventeen inbound flights.

Stranded passengers wait outside a Los Angeles International Airport (LAX) terminal after a series of events triggered a bomb scare in September 2004.

Shutting down LAX was understandable because a serious terrorist bomb plot, similar to the September 11, 2001, attacks on the World Trade Center, had been foiled on New Year's Eve 2000. On July 4, 2002, a mentally ill man sympathetic to terrorists began shooting at an LAX check-in counter. When the gunfire finally stopped, three people were dead.

Other bomb scare misunderstandings have a hidden humorous side. On December 24, 2003, the Brunswick Golden Isles Airport in Georgia was shut down after Transportation Safety Administration officials discovered an abandoned Christmas present. According to the Associated Press, the present's gift tag read, "Merry Christmas . . . This is not a bomb." Officials evacuated and sealed the airport, bringing in a robot to handle the package. After carefully examining, X-raying, and opening the package, it was discovered to contain a heavy glass candlestick from a local gift shop.

"It appears that this was an unwanted Christmas present," FBI special agent Tony Alig told the Associated Press. "Possibly thinking it was too good to throw in the trash, somebody left it where it would be found."

CHAPTER FOUR

What to Do in a Bomb Scare

On May 19, 2003, a real-life version of the movie *Speed* occurred near Washington, D.C. *Speed* told the story of a city bus rigged with a bomb set to explode as soon as the bus's speed fell below 50 miles (80.46 km) an hour.

In the real-life incident, twenty-four-year-old truck driver Joseph Reed was driving an eighteen-wheel truck full of paper products along the Beltway, a freeway encircling Washington, D.C. At about 11:30 AM, Reed had stopped at a convenience store for a soft drink and then had gotten back on the Beltway. A few minutes later, he was ready to cross the Woodrow Wilson Bridge when traffic slowed. During the slowdown, a car with male passengers pulled up next to his truck and yelled a dire warning: Someone had put explosives in his truck while he stopped at the store.

Then, the two men said that if Reed stopped his truck's engine again, the bomb would detonate.

At 11:35 AM, he called 911 from his truck. As he crossed the bridge, his truck crossed into Virginia. State trooper vehicles pulled in front of and behind the truck. More troopers and Virginia State Park Police cleared a safe area of the parkway. The troopers shut down the parkway and cleared all traffic. Reed pulled his truck to a stop on the empty parkway and ran to safety on the dispatcher's cue.

Using robots and bomb-sniffing dogs, officers searched the truck and found no explosives. The parkway was shut down for three hours, but fortunately, no one was hurt.

"In this day and age," Virginia State Park Police sergeant Scott Fear told the *Washington Post*, "you get a complaint like this, it's got to be taken seriously."

Reed's actions are a great example to follow in case of a bomb scare emergency. He stayed calm, immediately contacted authorities, and followed their instructions exactly. He didn't take any chances: he took the threat seriously. As Fear said, a threat of explosives has to be taken seriously.

What to Do in Case of Potential Danger

What if you are in a bomb scare? When and where the incident occurs is important. If you are in school, you probably have been through a number of bomb drills already. Still, follow your teacher's instructions and evacuate using your school's safety plan. If the school chooses to lock down while a threat is evaluated, remain calm. A "lockdown" means that all classrooms and other areas are secured. No one may leave until the danger has been identified and dealt with. Most often, schools lock down when there is an intruder in the building or a threatening person from outside may have entered the school.

Above all, safety professionals urge students not to gossip or speculate on what's going on beyond what teachers and administrators have said to everyone via the student address system. For example, the Wayne Valley High School smoke bomb scare discussed in this book's introduction became a lot worse for many students when someone suggested that the bombs were planted by terrorists.

Here are some important safety tips combined from guidelines prepared by the Federal Transportation Administration,

Students are guarded during a September 2005 school safety lockdown at Alamogordo High School in New Mexico.

the New York State Homeland Security System for Schools, and the Los Angeles Police Department bomb squad.

Telephone Threats

If you receive a bomb threat via the telephone at home, immediately hang up and go to a neighbor's or friend's house

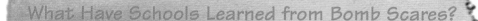

What Have Schools Learned from Bomb Scares?

Following the Columbine, Colorado, high school shootings (and bombings) in 1999, schools, students, and parents have been more concerned about safety than ever.

Some things have changed. The most immediate response to bomb threats or other violent school incidents in the past was evacuation. A student discussion following a bomb scare at Golden West High School in Visalia, California, in May 2004 brought to light that students might be safer remaining in their classrooms than evacuating immediately, before the threat has been evaluated.

A sophomore at Golden West High School sent two letters to the school and to the *Fresno Bee* newspaper threatening to blow up the school and kill several popular students. The threats caused the school to close for a day until the student was arrested and an investigation was conducted.

Teachers saw no warning signs that the student was upset, had been teased, or posed any type of threat. "It was tough because he was a great kid," history teacher Tony Casares told the *Fresno Bee*. "I felt like I missed something. It made me sick to my stomach."

Students and teachers met to talk about how to watch for signs of violence or anger that could lead to a bomb threat or a real attack. They also discussed a frightening incident that happened two weeks earlier at nearby Green Acres Middle School. The school had been closed for two days after a teacher found a threatening letter with white powder inside. Police and fire officials treated the powder as potentially deadly anthrax until a seventh-grader confessed that he had crushed some chalk and put it in an envelope to scare his friends.

Students agreed that they needed to be more aware of warning signs, and they said they should not be afraid to speak up if any of them saw or heard anything wrong or out of the ordinary. Teachers and students discussed better campus safety plans and improving communications, such as installing phones in all classrooms and using cell phones in case of an emergency. The most important priority for students and teachers after these incidents was one that can work in any school: good communication. Before a threat to prevent it from happening and in the case of a threat being received, communication promotes safety and can prevent injuries.

Surveillance photos show Eric Harris and Dylan Klebold during the Columbine High School shooting rampage in April 1999.

if possible. Once you're there, call 911 using a conventional house phone, not a cell phone. A cell phone is sometimes used deliberately to detonate bombs. Cell phones use radio signals that can unintentionally detonate a bomb. All schools have safety plans in case of telephone bomb threats. If you receive such a call while at school, immediately notify school authorities so

Airport security procedures and public warnings were posted after a suspicious package was found at Los Angeles International Airport (LAX) in February 2002.

they can initiate their plan. Try to remember as many details as you can about the caller's voice, and listen, if possible, for any background noise that could identify the caller's location.

Finding a Potential Bomb

Bombs can come in many forms. Airport and transportation security personnel are strict about passengers not leaving bags or backpacks unattended because bombs are easily hidden in these items. At other times, you may find an unconcealed device that looks like it could be a bomb.

If you see any bag, piece of luggage, or package unattended in an out-of-the-way location, treat it with caution. Do not attempt to open or touch the item to see what it is. Immediately notify the authorities and move a safe distance away. About 2,000 feet (610 meters) is the recommended distance.

Other potential bombs include thermoses, propane or other fuel canisters, and fire extinguishers. You may find objects that look very suspicious. Open bombs will have visible wires, batteries, and a clock or timer, and can have bottles, tanks, or bags attached. Boxes, bags, or packages emitting strong odors, mists, or oily liquids are also dangerous. Never pick up a discarded bottle filled with unusually colored liquid or that has strange objects inside. Never attempt to touch or remove a suspicious bottle in a mailbox or similar location.

As with a telephone threat received at home, do not use a cell phone to call 911 when you are near a suspected bomb. Evacuate the location and use a conventional telephone to call for help. Never, ever touch or attempt to investigate a suspected bomb on your own. The danger is far too great.

Encountering Suspicious Activity

You may be on a bus or walking down the street when you see something unusual. Forms of suspicious activity that can signal a bomb threat include:

- People acting strangely or talking about bombs or explosions
- Unattended cars or trucks parked in unusual locations
- Utility or repair crews that suddenly appear outside of construction zones
- Delivery trucks that aren't making deliveries
- People lurking on rooftops or in alleys
- People placing packages or bags at bus stops or terminals, then abandoning them

If you see any of this activity, and—as law enforcement professionals recommend, something doesn't seem right—leave the area and notify authorities as quickly as possible. Do not attempt to contact or confront any suspicious people you may see. If you see someone abandon a bag or package in a suspicious way, leave the area as quickly as possible. If you are riding on a bus or other public transportation, notify the driver so that he or she can initiate safety procedures.

General Safety Practices

Remember the basic safety rules. Don't forget that cell phones or walkie-talkies, which also use radio signals, could detonate a bomb. Protect yourself and others by evacuating the area as quickly and safely as possible. Follow your school's safety

If you see something, say something.

If you see an unattended bag, package or are witnessing suspicious activity on public transport, don't keep it to yourself.

Tell a staff member, or phone the Police on **000**.

Prominent security warnings were posted at the Sydney, Australia, airport in 2005 after the London subway and Madrid train bombings.

plan if an incident occurs at school. Never try to confront a suspicious person on your own. Remember any details of threats or suspicious activity to the best of your ability—it could be the key to saving lives later on.

Above all, remain calm. Don't forget that people can be hurt if they evacuate in a disorganized way. Don't forget that others may misunderstand what you say, and a plastic soda bottle bomb could turn into a terrorist attack by the time many people have shared the information.

At school, other students may have disabilities, may not understand the danger, or may not know about the safety plan. If you know the basic rules, you can save your own life and the lives of many others in the case of a bomb scare.

CHAPTER FIVE
What the Future Holds

Although bomb threats and scares are becoming more frequent, chances are you will never be involved in a serious incident. Even so, almost everyone is familiar with bomb scares and has probably thought about what would happen if he or she was in one. High-profile bomb scares like the *Aqua Teen Hunger Force* ad campaign in Boston, or real terrorist attacks such as the train bombings in Madrid, Spain, give today's bomb scares a greater impact than they've ever had before.

In addition to news reports of bomb scares and bombings, bomb scares and threats are a major feature in the plots of many television shows and films. Television shows, ranging from *Numb3rs* to *Criminal Minds* to *24*, have featured plots about bombs, threats, and bombers with many different motivations, from political terrorists to disturbed firefighters or police officers who set off bombs.

The real circumstances behind some bomb plots are even more suspenseful and complex that a fictional television show or movie. One such circumstance is the fifteen-year manhunt for the Unabomber, Ted Kaczynski. However, law enforcement officials say that bombs aren't glamorous and suspenseful in real life. Bomb threats and pranks are never funny when played out in reality. Bombs can kill, and the fear inspired during a bomb prank or hoax can cause a trauma reaction in innocent victims that could last for years.

Understanding the difference between real life and entertainment is important in trying to understand the impact of bomb scares on our lives. Experts who work in the field of bomb technology, safety, and security have some surprising predictions about what types of bombs and bomb scares are likely to become more common in the future. Most surprising of all, the future of bomb scares isn't high tech, according to experts. The bombs of the future are much more likely to be made by the average Joe in a garage than by James Bond–type villains.

Future Scares and Threats

It's a sad fact, but bomb squads in major cities receive more bomb threats after any major international terrorist attack. These tragedies inspire copycats, pranksters, and hoaxers.

Members of major city bomb squads like the Los Angeles Police Department (LAPD) bomb squad are the experts. They train around the world for virtually any type of threat that might occur in their city. The biggest high-tech future terrorist attacks could be biological (bombs releasing deadly diseases, like anthrax), nuclear (especially dirty bombs, which do not produce a large explosion but do produce a lot of invisible, deadly radiation), or chemical (bombs releasing deadly poisons like nerve gas).

When they're not responding to bomb threats, bomb squad technicians, which in major cities can include officers with chemistry and engineering degrees, practice their skills by making dummy bombs and quickly disarming them. Or they help to train their bomb-sniffing dogs, or K9s.

John Miller is the commander of the Los Angeles Police Department's Counter-Terrorism Bureau (CTB) and bomb

A Florida security officer trains a three-year-old Labrador retriever named Duke to detect explosives in January 2002.

squad. Miller is a former television news reporter and New York City police commissioner. He is an expert in bombs and terrorist threats. The LAPD bomb squad office is filled with confiscated explosives, ranging from crude and strange-looking homemade devices to grenades and even rocket launchers that were found in the attic of a Los Angeles home. Miller told the *Los Angeles Times* that the biggest increase in bomb threats was likely to come not from sophisticated terrorist attacks, such as biological or nuclear weapons, but from homegrown bombs that could be made from common household items.

John Miller and many other bomb experts agree that the Internet plays a major role in inspiring bomb scares. Web sites and Internet videos distribute information that could inspire, or inform, potential bombers, criminals who might make false or extortion threats, and pranksters.

By building bombs from simple, common ingredients, terrorists and criminals could, as one bomb squad detective told the *Los Angeles Times*, get more bang for their buck.

Most bomb experts also agree that terrorist attacks like the 2004 Madrid, Spain, train bombings, and the July 2005 subway bombings in London, England, have a strong potential of occurring in the United States. Many local and national officials who have been charged with combating terrorism have said that it's not a matter of if such an attack will occur in the United States—it's a matter of when.

What Does This Mean to You?

By following safety tips and acting wisely, you will know the right thing to do if you are ever confronted with a bomb scare.

A federal Transportation Safety Administration (TSA) airport security screener uses X-ray and other technology at Atlanta International Airport in 2003.

You might even be like the student at Wayne Valley High School who identified the smoke bombs in the school's lockers before they went off. His actions stopped a poorly thought-out prank that could have had unintentional deadly results. While the students who thought the smoke bomb prank was a good idea got into a lot of trouble, they would have been in a lot more trouble if anyone had actually gotten hurt.

If you are involved in a bomb scare or disaster, and you are experiencing feelings of fear, trauma, and distress as a result, remember that help is always available. Never feel reluctant to talk to your family, friends, teachers, or counselors about how you are feeling. Many organizations, from the American Red Cross to the American Psychological Association, have resources for bomb scare survivors and other disaster survivors.

Although bomb scares can make anyone feel helpless, you can still be prepared. What steps can you follow to be prepared? First, by reading this book, you are more informed and prepared than you were before. Second, all schools and districts have safety plans, and nearly all of these plans have safety procedures to follow in the event of a bomb scare.

The way you will prepare is as unique as you are. Think of other situations where you planned ahead of time. If you play sports, you figure things out while you are practicing. If you are a musician, dancer, actor, or artist, you practice before a performance or you make sketches to learn how to draw different things before you start a final picture. Even if you don't do any of these things, you are still a student—and you know how much better it is when you study and prepare before a test than if you don't.

Students console each other after the tragic April 1999 attacks at Columbine High School in Littleton, Colorado.

Sports, music, dancing, acting, and art are all positive activities. Bomb scares are the exact opposite. Most people would never want to face such a potentially deadly event. But by working together and communicating well, all of us can prepare, save lives, and survive a bomb scare or threat.

anarchist bomber A politically motivated bomber that emerged in the nineteenth century in Europe.

anthrax A potentially deadly bacteria that can be weaponized by turning its spores (the bacteria in its dormant form) into a powder than can be inhaled or cause infections through the skin.

biological bomb A device that contains an infectious disease that is released on detonation, or a package that contains a dangerous disease in powdered form, such as anthrax.

C-4 Also known as Composition 4, it is one of the most common and powerful types of plastic explosives. It can be molded into any shape and remains stable until detonated.

chemical bomb A bomb that releases deadly chemicals, such as nerve gas, upon detonation.

detonation The act of exploding a bomb. Bomb squads deliberately detonate bombs in a safe environment to save lives.

dirty bomb Also called an RDD or radiological dispersal device, a dirty bomb releases poisonous radiation through a conventional (non-nuclear) explosion that distributes the radioactive material.

EOD K-9 An explosive ordnance disposal canine, or bomb-sniffing dog.

evacuation The law enforcement and safety term for the process of safely leaving an area that has received a threat.

extortion The legal term for threatening someone with violence in order to obtain money or property. Bomb threats are used as extortion techniques by criminals.

grenadiers Seventeenth-century European soldiers who received special training to use grenades, one of the earliest forms of bombs.

IED An improvised explosive device, which has been used against U.S. troops in the conflicts in Iraq and Afghanistan.

lockdown The procedure schools follow to ensure students stay safely in their classrooms when there is an outside threat.

lockout A school safety procedure that prevents outsiders from entering a school during periods of danger.

mine A land or water mine is an explosive device that is buried in the ground or placed in the water. Mines detonate with pressure or contact, or they can be remotely detonated with a radio or other devices.

ordnance In general, an ordnance can mean any type of military supply or equipment. It can also be dangerous and explosive ammunition such as grenades, shells, land mines, or missiles.

perpetrator A term used primarily by law enforcement to describe a person who has committed a crime.

shrapnel Hot metal shards that cause serious injuries in a bomb or grenade explosion.

Department of Justice Canada
284 Wellington Street
Ottawa, ON K1A 0H8
Canada
(613) 957-4207
Web site: http://justicecanada.ca
The Department of Justice Canada offers information on Canada's
Anti-Terrorism Act (ATA) and assistance for victims, including those
of bomb scares.

National Mental Health Association
2000 North Beauregard Street, 6th Floor
Alexandria, VA 22311
(800) 969-6642
Web site: http://www.nmha.org
The National Mental Health Association provides information for coping
with and recovering from trauma and disasters, including bomb scares.

Royal Canadian Mounted Police (RCMP)
Canadian Bomb Data Centre
RCMP Public Affairs and Communications Services
Headquarters Building
1200 Vanier Parkway
Ottawa, ON K1A 0R2
Canada
(613) 993-7267
Web site: http://www.rcmp-grc.gc.ca/techops/cbdc/index_e.htm
The RCMP Canadian Bomb Data Centre provides complete information on
how to respond to bomb threats, as well as information on Canadian bomb
statistics and bomb squad activities.

U.S. Department of Homeland Security (DHS)
Washington, DC 20528
(202) 282-8000
Web site: http://www.dhs.gov
The DHS provides information on prevention and protection, and preparedness and response, for a wide range of disasters, including bomb scares and threats.

Web Sites

Due to the changing nature of Internet links, Rosen Publishing has developed an online list of Web sites related to the subject of this book. This site is updated regularly. Please use this link to access the list:

http://www.rosenlinks.com/vas/bosc

Cooney, Caroline. *The Terrorist*. New York, NY: Scholastic, 1999.

Gerstein, Ted, and Richard Esposito. *Bomb Squad: A Year Inside the Nation's Most Exclusive Police Unit*. New York, NY: Hyperion, 2007.

Gonzalez, Lisette. *Bomb Squads in Action* (Dangerous Jobs). New York, NY: PowerKids Press, 2007.

Holliday, Laurel. *Why Do They Hate Me? Young Lives Caught in War and Conflict*. New York, NY: Simon Pulse, 1999.

Pratchett, Terry. *Johnny and the Bomb*. New York, NY: HarperCollins, 2007.

Shapiro, Larry. *Special Police Vehicles*. Osceola, WI: Motorbooks International, 1999.

Stein, Tammar. *Light Years: A Novel*. New York, NY: Knopf Books for Young Readers, 2005.

BIBLIOGRAPHY

Alexander, Andrea, and Michael Feeney. "Five Graduates Face Bomb Scare Charges." *Bergen Record*. June 28, 2007, p. 1.

The American National Red Cross. *Masters of Disaster Series* (Be Disaster Safe Level 3). Washington, DC. American Red Cross, 2007.

Croft, Pauline. "Gunpowder Plot: Pauline Croft Explains the Origins of Bonfire Night by Reconstructing Events 400 Years Ago." *History Review*. September 1, 2005.

Doege, David. "Post-Columbine Bomb Scare Cases End Up Misdemeanors." *Milwaukee Journal-Sentinel*. April 7, 2000, p. 3.

Feeney, Michael. "Bomb Scare Culprits Captured on Video." *Bergen Record*. June 15, 2007, p. 1.

Feeney, Michael. "Pomp, Circumstance After Bomb Scare." *Bergen Record*. June 22, 2007, p. 1.

Feeney, Michael. "Task Force Will Probe Bomb Scare." *Bergen Record*. June 21, 2007, p. 1.

Gerstein, Ted, and Richard Esposito. *Bomb Squad: A Year Inside the Nation's Most Exclusive Police Unit*. New York, NY: Hyperion, 2007.

Jackman, Tom. "A Truck Bomb Scare, Hollywood Style; Parkway Closed in Hoax Similar to Plot of Movie." *Washington Post*. May 20, 2003, p. 3.

Los Angeles Police Protective League. "A Good Day for the Bomb Squad Is No Blast." Retrieved December 18, 2007 Reprint of *Los Angeles Times* article. Retrieved September 5, 2007. (http://www.lapd.com/article.aspx?&a=2938).

Los Angeles Police Department. "History and Overview of the Bomb Squad." Retrieved December 18, 2007 (http://www.lapdonline.org/emergency_services_division/content_basic_view/6523).

Personal Interview. Detective John Wills, Los Angeles Police Department Special Operations, Bomb Squad. September 19, 2007.

Personal Interview. Alex Williams, Cody Marks and Meredith Casil – Redlands East Valley High School students. September 4, 2007.

Plemons, Jason D. "Bomb Scares Close Golden West. Two Letters Lead to Visalia Campus's Closure Today." *Fresno Bee*. May 19, 2004, p. 1.

Smith, Jim. *A Law Enforcement and Security Officer's Guide to Responding to Bomb Threats: Providing Working Knowledge of Bombs, Preparing for Such Incidents, and Performing Basic Analysis of Potential Threats*. Springfield, IL: C.C. Thomas, 2003.

Shapiro, Bruce. "A Rational Unabomber? (The Trial of Theodore Kaczynski Calls Attention to the Fact that up to 15% of U.S. Inmates Have Mental Disorders)." *The Nation*. January 28, 1998.

Thurman, James T. *Practical Bomb Scene Investigation*. Boca Raton, FL: CRC Press, 2006.

United States Department of Education. *Practical Information on Crisis Planning: A Guide for Schools and Communities*. Washington, DC: 2004.

University of the State of New York, State Education Department. *New York State Homeland Security System for Schools*. Revised Edition. Albany, NY: 2003.

INDEX

About the Author

Amy Sterling Casil is an award-nominated writer. She has published seventeen books, including *Coping with Terrorism* published by the Rosen Publishing Group, which began her research into bomb scares and safety plans. She has a master's degree in creative writing and literature from Chapman University in Orange, California, and taught composition and literature in Southern California schools for six years. Her experience teaching all levels of college reading and writing contributed to the success of her extensive fiction, nonfiction, and poetry writing for grades K–12 for McGraw-Hill and other educational publishers. She lives in Redlands, California, with her daughter, a high school student, and serves in an executive position for Beyond Shelter, a nationally recognized Los Angeles organization providing affordable housing and programs for homeless families.

Photo Credits

Cover (foreground left) © Ian Waldie/Getty Images, (foreground right) © Mustafa Ozer/AFP/Getty Images, (background) © Spencer Platt/Getty Images; p. 1 © www.istockphoto.com/ranplett; pp. 4, 10, 18, 22, 24, 26, 30, 32, 35, 39, 41, 42, 49, 51 © AP Images; p. 12 © Hulton Archive/Getty Images; p. 13 © Mario Tama/Getty Images; p. 15 © Bettmann/Corbis; p. 29 © Darren McCollester/Getty Images; p. 45 © Greg Wood/AFP/Getty Images; p. 53 © Mark Leffingwell/AFP/Getty Images.

Designer: Nelson Sá; **Editor:** Nicholas Croce;
Photo Researcher: Amy Feinberg